Puma

Jaguar

Cheetah

Persian Cat

In this book, renowned artist Eric Carle follows a young boy
in his search for his cat, introducing members of the greater
cat family at the same time. Using his brilliant collages,
Mr. Carle again creates a world both childlike and touching
in this miniature version of his classic tale especially
designed for the very young.

Other Eric Carle books available in miniature:
The Very Hungry Caterpillar
The Very Busy Spider

Have You Seen My Cat?

by Eric Carle

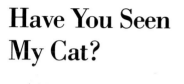

Hamish Hamilton

Have you seen my cat?

This is
not *my*
cat!

Have you seen my cat?

This is not *my* cat!

Have you seen my cat?

This is not

my cat!

Have you
seen my cat?

This is not *my* cat!

Have you
seen my cat?

This is not *my* cat!

Have you
seen my cat?

This is not *my* cat!

Have you seen my cat?

This is not *my* cat!

Have you seen my cat?

This is not *my* cat!

Where is my cat?

Have you seen my cat?

This is my cat!

Dedicated to all the cats in my life

Also available in miniature:
The Very Hungry Caterpillar   The Very Busy Spider

HAMISH HAMILTON CHILDREN'S BOOKS

Published by the Penguin Group
27 Wrights Lane, London W8 5TZ, England
Viking Penguin Inc, 40 West 23rd Street, New York, New York 10010, U.S.A.
Penguin Books Australia Ltd, Ringwood, Victoria, Australia
Penguin Books Canada Ltd, 2801 John Street, Markham, Ontario, Canada L3R 1B4
Penguin Books (N.Z.) Ltd, 182-190 Wairau Road, Auckland 10, New Zealand

Penguin Books Ltd, Registered Offices: Harmondsworth, Middlesex, England

Full size edition first published in Great Britain 1988
by Holder and Stoughton Children's Books
This miniature edition first published in Great Britain 1989 by Hamish Hamilton Children's Books

Copyright © 1973, 1988 by Eric Carle Corp., 1988
1 3 5 7 9 10 8 6 4 2

British Library Cataloguing in Publication Data
CIP data for this book is available from the British Library

ISBN 0-241-12492-1

Lion

Bobcat

Panther

Tiger